To my wife, Marla; our children, Omar-Sol and Sophia;
and my mother, Gigi Gregory
—W.P.

For Ruth E. Edwards
—R.G.C.

Text copyright © 2024 by William Wylie
Jacket art and interior illustrations copyright © 2024 by R. Gregory Christie

All rights reserved. Published in the United States by Crown Books for Young Readers, an imprint of
Random House Children's Books, a division of Penguin Random House LLC, New York.
Original version entitled IN THE WEST END created in collaboration with Alliance Theatre
and the Mayor's Summer Reading Club of Atlanta, Georgia.

Crown and the colophon are registered trademarks of Penguin Random House LLC.

Visit us on the Web! rhcbooks.com

Educators and librarians, for a variety of teaching tools, visit us at RHTeachersLibrarians.com

Library of Congress Cataloging-in-Publication Data is available upon request.
ISBN 978-0-593-65239-8 (trade) — ISBN 978-0-593-65240-4 (lib. bdg.) — ISBN 978-0-593-65241-1 (ebook)

The text of this book is set in 16-point Whale Song regular.
The illustrations in this book were created using Acryla Gouache.

Book design by Véronique Lefèvre Sweet

MANUFACTURED IN CHINA

10 9 8 7 6 5 4 3 2 1

First Edition

Nana's New Soul Food

Written by **Will Power**

Illustrated by **R. Gregory Christie**

Crown Books for Young Readers ♔ New York

I like pizza!
I like pancakes!
I like barbecued and fried and stewed chicken.
I like popcorn with lots of salt and sugar.
And peach cobbler.
And ham hocks and Pop Rocks!

My nana, she makes it all!
(Well, not the Pop Rocks. Nana doesn't make those,
but she'll buy them for me.)

Her food is sooooo yummy.

And I always have fun with Nana.
I love her. . . .

But now Nana is sick.

She can't eat the same foods that she used to—
the things she loves to make,
the food she loves to eat.

Her favorite foods are my favorite, too!

But the doctor says she has to change what she eats
if she wants to be happy and see me graduate.

Nana has to eat differently.
So . . .

. . . Momma and I set out to find tasty treats that she can eat.

We walk through the West End.

We go to Queen Wraps,
with their big ol' green and red wraps
stuffed with couscous
and this thing like spinach called kale.

We get one, so Nana can taste one.

So much healthy food
(Momma says delicious food—
I say healthy food)
in the West End.

We go to a buffet
where the gravy is savory like Nana's.

But the gravy is made of mushrooms! Really?
I don't even like mushrooms, but I like this.

There's yumminess in the West End.

Momma, do you think Nana
would like this mac and cheese?

They say it's no cow used to make it,
a nut blend that fakes it.

Can I have a taste?
Mmm . . . scrumptious. Nana might like this.

Or how about a veggie burger
with lots of ketchup?

The line is long. . . .
How long will it take
to catch up to the front?

Fries too, Momma,
but air-popped, not deep-fried.
The doctor said Nana can't
have deep-fried anymore.

I miss Nana's cooking.
Momma, is she going to be okay?
"Yes, baby," Momma says.
"Let's get her something to eat."

We go through the West End.
So much delicious food
(Momma says healthy food—
I say delicious food)
in the West End.

We stop at the Juice Bar for a juice and a—
How do you say it, Momma? Veg-in? What's a veg-in?

"Vegan, baby. Vegan donut."

Tasty donuts, they should call them.
And so many choices—wow!

What if we stacked those donuts
one on top of the other
and made a tall donut castle?

Donuts, in the West End.

Momma, do you think Nana will like
this yummy food?
I hope she does.

"I'm sure she will. I hope she will."

Imagine a world where everything's healthy . . .
where delicious food is good for you, too.

Momma, can you see?
In the West End they have new soul food.

One last place to go—the farmer's market!
There are all kinds of fruits.

Look, Momma—juicy bright-purple grapes,
green, green spinach (not a fruit, but it still looks good),
and oranges like the moon.
Can we get some, Momma?

"Yes, let's use this bag that I brought."

Yay! I can't wait to give this food to Nana!

Look, Nana. Look!
We got you some mac and cheese,
a big ol' yummy red wrap,
a veggie burger and fries—
wait till you try the fries and the burger—
and a juice and donuts and fruit and . . .

Nana, I know you're going to like these new foods!

And pretty soon, just imagine,
you can make your own kind of
new soul food.

Like kale salad, Nana—that would hit the spot.
And veggie burgers, with pickles piled high on top.

I don't know if we can make vegan Pop Rocks.
But maybe something tastier,
like mango coconut pops?

Can we make them, Nana?

"Sure. . . . This is all new to me, though.
How about we make them together?"

Yeah! You and me!
We'll make the best food. Just like in the West End!

I love you, Nana.

"I love you, too, baby."

Author's Note

Dear Readers,

This book is about the power of our younger generations and how they are introducing ideas of plant-based eating to their parents and grandparents. I wanted to write a book in which the protagonist is on a mission to save his grandmother and preserve his family. Though he may not be aware of it, his actions are part of a global movement, and countless conversations are occurring within communities right now. How do we retain the joys of our culinary heritage while attempting to eat healthier? How do we make more nutritious and eco-friendly meals? Throughout the world, young people are initiating these conversations. They are truly leading the way.

And yet, this transition to healthier eating and living has to be embraced by the older members of our families. So I am dedicating *Nana's New Soul Food* to the young people, such as the precocious boy in this tale, and to the chefs, parents, and nanas throughout the world who are working together to reimagine delicious cultural foods in healthier ways.

Nana's New Soul Food is also a love letter to Atlanta, a city where this kind of reimagining is in full demand, with plant-based eateries and vegan soul food joints popping up in so many places. And still, this book reflects not only Atlanta but all neighborhoods and cities where people are trying to do things differently when it comes to the health of those they love.

Mango-Coconut-Lime Ice Pops
Courtesy of Chef Bryant Terry

Yield: Makes 12 ice pops

Ingredients:

1 cup coconut milk

2 ½ teaspoons lime zest

2 tablespoons raw cane sugar

4 large ripe mangoes (about 12 ounces each), peeled, pitted, and roughly chopped

4 tablespoons freshly squeezed lime juice

6 tablespoons freshly squeezed orange juice

Instructions:

- With a grown-up's help or supervision, combine the coconut milk and the lime zest in a small saucepan and simmer over medium-low heat, stirring often, until the coconut milk has reduced to half a cup, about 10 minutes.

- Transfer the reduced coconut milk to an upright blender, add the remaining ingredients, and purée until smooth. Pour the mixture into ice pop molds, leaving ¼ inch space at the top to allow for expansion after freezing. Place the pops in a freezer until completely frozen, at least 8 hours or overnight.

- To unmold, gently squeeze each pop as you pull the handle. If it does not release, run the molds under warm water for a few seconds and try again.